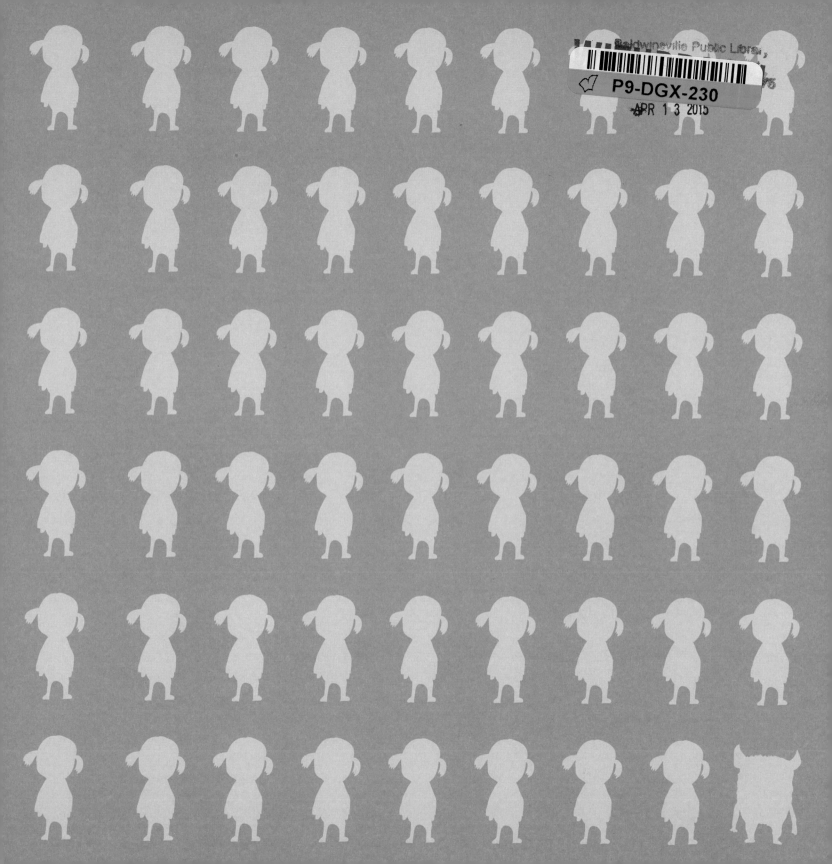

SANTI BALMES   pictures by LYONA

I Will Fight MONSTERS for You

ALBERT WHITMAN & COMPANY
CHICAGO, ILLINOIS

It was pouring rain outside and Martina was scared. The night had come. When the moon appeared, Martina knew she would be sent to bed. Her parents would go to sleep in their room. Even the television would go quiet and start to snore.

Nobody, except her, would hear the MONSTER...

Martina was sure there was a city of MONSTERS living on the other side of her bedroom floor in an upside-down world.

Everything in the whole world, thought Martina, had its own upside-down monster reflection.

Just like this picture!

Sometimes Martina had nightmares
that all the MONSTERS jumped up
and down at the same time.

They would make the floor cave in
and give everyone a terrible fright!

That night, Martina could not sleep. She was
sure that if she left her arm hanging over
the side of her bed, the monster would make
a hole in the floor, grab her hand, and maybe
pull her into the monster world where she
would have to learn how to live upside down.
The MONSTER might even make Martina
learn how to scare people!

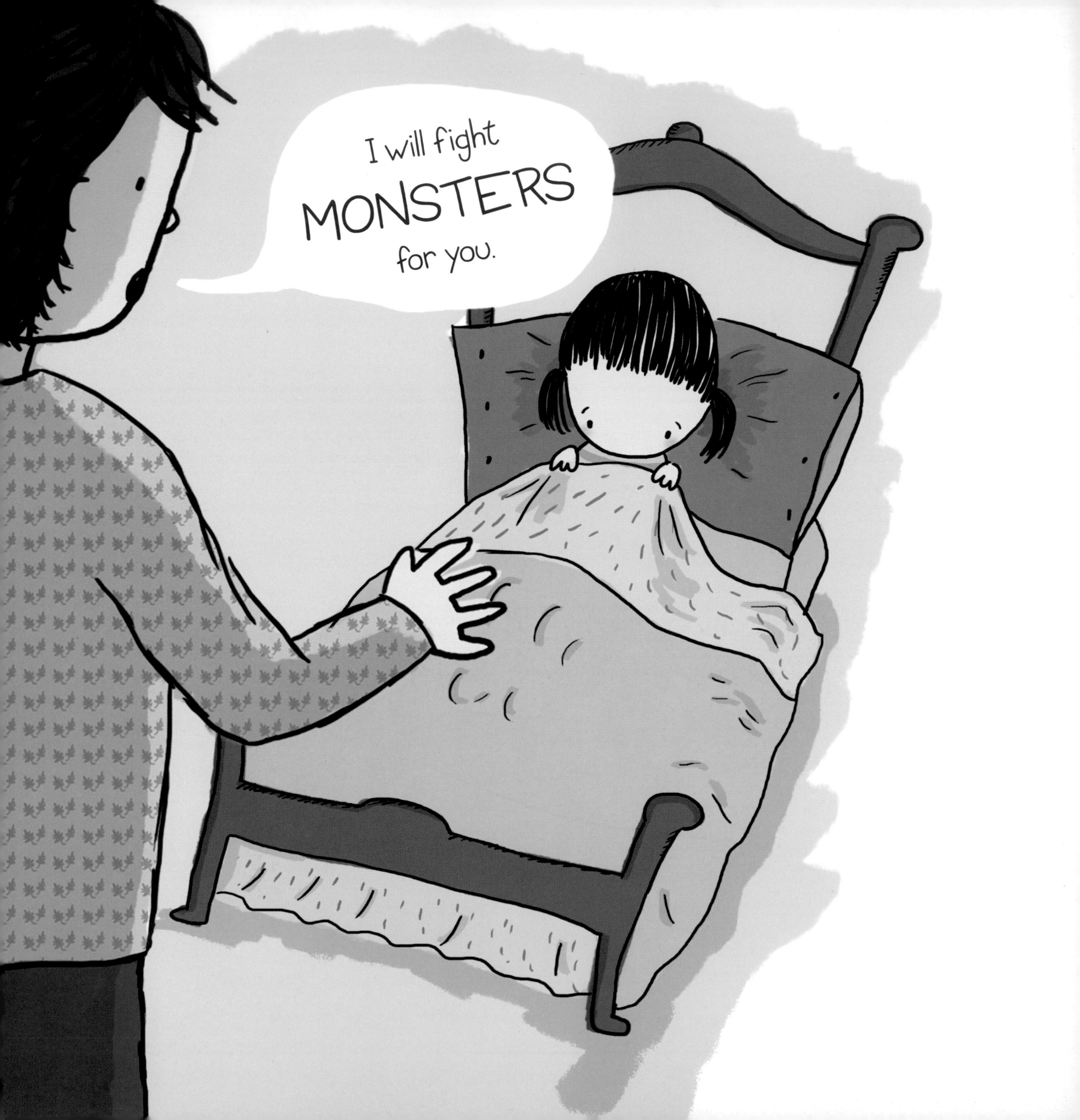
I will fight
MONSTERS
for you.

She was so afraid that she lay very still, making sure that not one inch of her body was outside her bed sheets. And then she called her daddy.

"How big do you think monsters are? What if the monster is as big as you? What will I do?"

"Call me," said her father. "I will fight MONSTERS for you."

"How?" Martina asked.

"I am an expert monster fighter. But I'll need your help. You must try to feel brave. The size of the MONSTERS depends on how scared you are. If you feel very brave, the monster will shrink and run away."

This made Martina feel better and before she knew it, she had fallen asleep.

Martina started dreaming about a
MONSTER girl. She was covered in
pink fur and her name was Anitram.

In the monster world, it was also raining. Anitram was scared. The night had come. When the moon appeared, Anitram knew she would be sent to bed. Her monster parents would go to their bedroom and fall asleep with their monster snores. Even the monster television would be snoring. Nobody, except her, would hear the HUMAN.

Anitram was convinced that on the other side of the floor was a human city. Everything in her world had its own upside-down reflection—the pink roads, the hairy houses, and even the blue trees. There were exactly as many HUMANS as there were monsters, so if there was to be a war, the fight would be quite equal, even though the monsters had strawberry shooters and giant pencils to defend themselves.

Anitram imagined that under her bed a HUMAN girl lived. They were the same age and were even born on the same day!

Anitram had heard the girl jumping on her bed—this human girl was very noisy. But what if all the HUMANS started jumping at the same time? They might make the floor cave in!

That night Anitram couldn't sleep. She was sure that the HUMAN girl would make a hole in the floor, grab her arm, and maybe pull her through to the HUMAN world. She would have to learn how to live upside down. The girl might even make Anitram learn how to scare monsters!

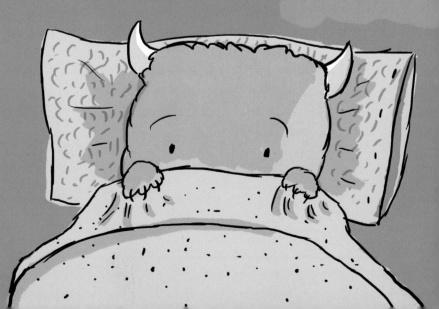

really big fear

She was so afraid that she lay very still, making sure that not one inch of her body was outside her bed sheets. And then she called her daddy.

"I can hear that noisy girl jumping on the bed! What if she's as big as you? What will I do?" Anitram asked.

"Call me," answered her father. "I will fight FEARS for you. Did you know that fear is elastic, like bubble gum? As you grow braver, fear shrinks smaller and smaller until it disappears."

This made Anitram feel better
and before she knew it,
she had fallen asleep.

teeny tiny fear

Anitram was so comfortable
that her arm slipped out from
under the bed sheets and hung
over the side of the bed.

At the exact same moment, Martina's arm fell from under her bed sheets toward the floor.

Nobody knows how it happened, but just then, an enormous hole appeared in the floor. It's just one of those magical things that happen while we dream.

The tips of Martina's fingers dangled into the hole and reached into the other world—the world she was so afraid of—the MONSTER world.

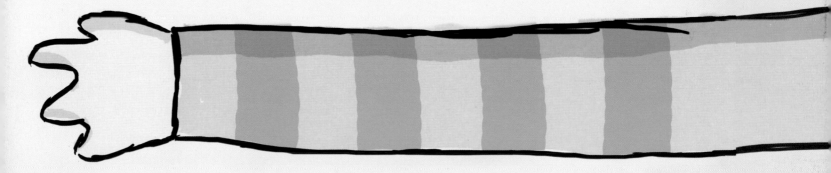

The same happened to the little MONSTER.

Both hands touched. Martina's hand felt warm and Anitram's was soft and fuzzy. They both realized that they had been scared of each other because they had never met. They knew they would not need their daddies to fight for them because there was nothing to be afraid of.

From then on, they never worried about what was under the bed at night.

GOOD NIGHT!

Library of Congress Cataloging-in-Publication
data is on file with the publisher.

Copyright © 2011 by Santi Balmes
Copyright © 2011 for illustrations by Lyona
Copyright © 2011 Principal de los Libros
Published by arrangement with The K Literary and Film agency.
Published in 2015 by Albert Whitman & Company
ISBN 978-0-8075-9056-0   APR 1 3 2015

Printed in China.
10 9 8 7 6 5 4 3 2 1 HH 18 17 16 15 14

For more information about Albert Whitman & Company,
visit our web site at www.albertwhitman.com.

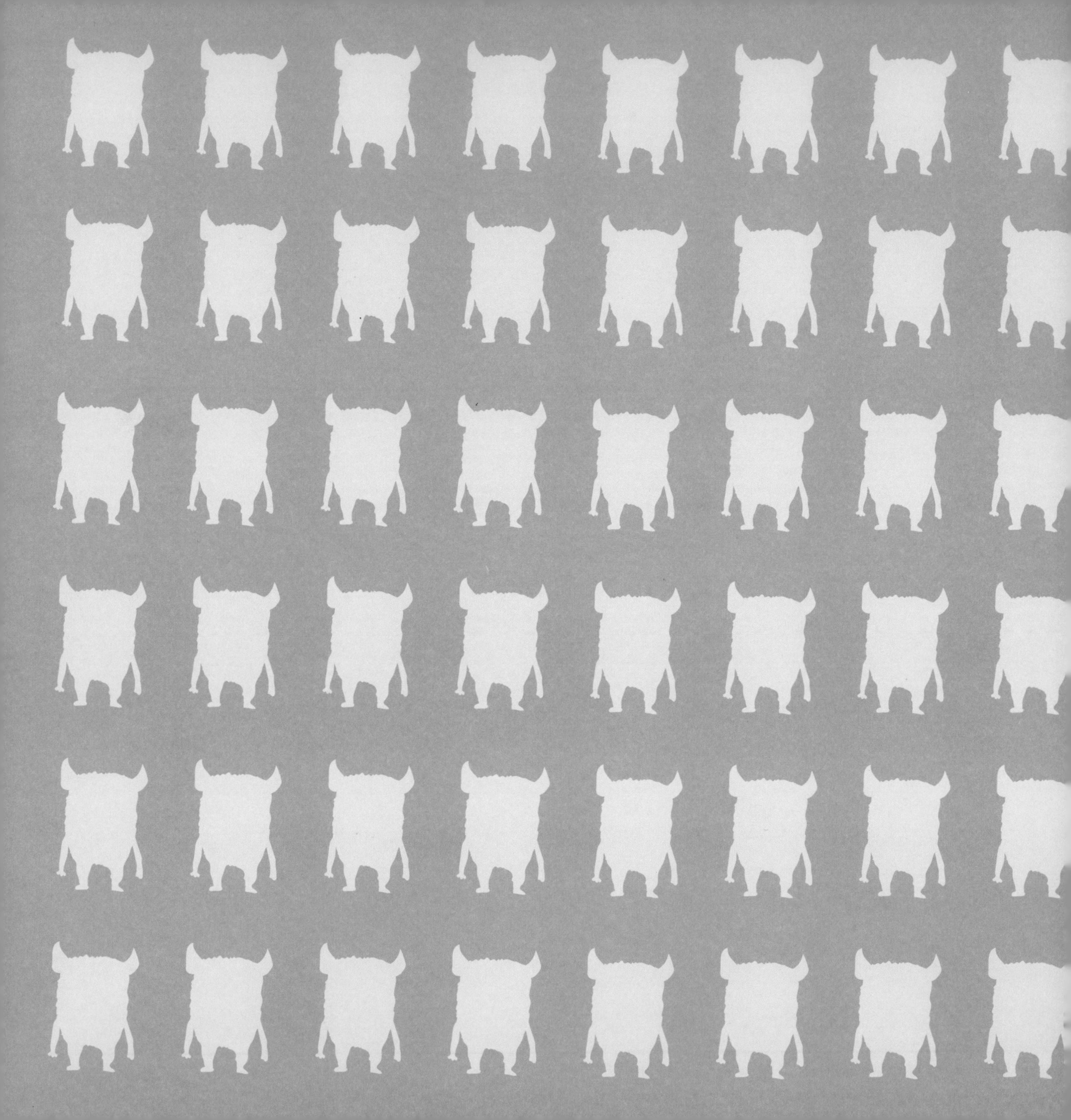